THE TRACTOR RACE

BY MARI SCHUH

AMICUS READERS 1 AMICUS INK

Say Hello to Amicus Readers.

You'll find our helpful dog, Amicus, chasing a ball—to let you know the reading level of a book.

1

Learn to Read

High frequency words and close photo-text matches introduce familiar topics and provide ample support for brand new readers.

2

Read Independently

Some repetition is mixed with varied sentence structures and a select amount of new vocabulary words are introduced with text and photo support.

3

Read to Know More

Interesting facts and engaging art and photos give fluent readers fun books both for reading practice and to learn about new topics.

Amicus Readers and Amicus Ink are imprints of Amicus
P.O. Box 227, Mankato, MN 56002
www.amicuspublishing.us

Library of Congress Cataloging-in-Publication Data
Names: Schuh, Mari C., 1975-
Title: The tractor race / by Mari Schuh.
Description: Mankato, Minnesota : Amicus, [2017] | Series: Let's race | Audience: Grades: K to Grade 3._
Identifiers: LCCN 2015044780 (print) | LCCN 2015047898 (ebook) | ISBN 9781607539162 (Library Binding) | ISBN 9781681510408 (eBook) | ISBN 9781681521367 (paperback)
Subjects: LCSH: Riding lawn mowers--Juvenile literature. | Racing--Juvenile literature. | Contests--Juvenile literature.
Classification: LCC SB433.2 .S24 2017 (print) | LCC SB433.2 (ebook) | DDC 629.228--dc23
LC record available at http://lccn.loc.gov/2015044780

Editor: Wendy Dieker
Designer: Tracy Myers
Photo Researcher: Aubrey Harper

Photo Credits: Ville Palonen/Alamy Stock Photo cover; LOOK-foto/Superstock 3; Stephen Bartholomew/Alamy Live News 4-5; Peter Steffen/epa/Corbis 7; Leo Mason sports photos/Alamy Stock Photo 8-9; Fir0002/Flagstaffotos 11, 15; John Jewell/Dreamstime 12-13; Stephen Power/Alamy Stock Photo 16

Printed in the United States of America.

Let's watch a lawn tractor race!

NGK
SPARK PLUGS
11
10

Vroom! Vroom!

The engines roar.

The race starts.

Dirt flies. The riders make many laps.

Ed tries to pass
Sue. Hold on!
Ed spins off
the track.

Leo keeps his
eyes on the track.
He is in the lead.
Go, Leo!

Gulf
36
Gulf

One lap to go!

Sue passes Mike.

The race is over.

Leo wins!

T155

PARTS OF A LAWN TRACTOR